D0202291
Old MacDonald
Had a Farm

Old MacDonald had a farm, **Ee i ee i oh!**
And on his farm he had lots of animals, **Ee i ee i oh!**
And they made **noise** here,
And they made **noise** there.
Here a **noise**, there a **noise**,
Everywhere there's **noisy noise**.
Old MacDonald had a farm, **Ee i ee i oh!**

Old MacDonald had a farm, **Ee i ee i oh!**
And on his farm he had a cow, **Ee i ee i oh!**

With a **moo-moo** here,
And a **moo-moo** there.

Here a **moo**, there a **moo**,

Everywhere a **moo-moo**.

Old MacDonald had a farm, Ee i ee i oh!

Old MacDonald had a farm, **Ee i ee i oh!**
And on his farm he had a pig, **Ee i ee i oh!**
With an **oink-oink** here,
And an **oink-oink** there.

Here an **oink**, there an **oink**,
Everywhere an **oink-oink**.
Old MacDonald had a farm, **Ee i ee i oh!**

Old MacDonald had a farm, **Ee i ee i oh!**
And on his farm he had some chicks, **Ee i ee i oh!**
With a **chirp-chirp** here,
And a **chirp-chirp** there.

Here a **chirp**, there a **chirp**,
Everywhere a **chirp-chirp**.
Old MacDonald had a farm, **Ee i ee i oh!**

Old MacDonald had a farm, **Ee i ee i oh!**
And on his farm he had a rooster, **Ee i ee i oh!**
With a **cock-a-doodle-doo** here,
And a **cock-a-doodle-doo** there.

Here a **doodle**, there a **doodle**,

Everywhere a **cock-a-doodle**.

Old MacDonald had a farm, **Ee i ee i oh!**

Old MacDonald had a farm, Ee i ee i oh!
And on his farm he had a lamb, Ee i ee i oh!
With a baa-baa here,
And a baa-baa there.

Here a **baa**, there a **baa**,
Everywhere a **baa-baa**.
Old MacDonald had a farm, **Ee i ee i oh!**

Old MacDonald had a farm, **Ee i ee i oh!**
And on his farm he had a cat, **Ee i ee i oh!**
With a **meow-meow** here,
And a **meow-meow** there.
Here a **meow**, there a **meow**,
Everywhere a **meow-meow**.
Old MacDonald had a farm, **Ee i ee i oh!**

Old MacDonald had a farm, Ee i ee i oh!
And on his farm he had a turkey, Ee i ee i oh!
With a gobble-gobble here,
And a gobble-gobble there.
Here a gobble, there a gobble,
Everywhere a gobble-gobble.

Old MacDonald had a farm, Ee i ee i oh!

Old MacDonald had a farm, **Ee i ee i oh!**

And on his farm he had a horse, **Ee i ee i oh!**

With a **neigh-neigh** here,

And a **neigh-neigh** there.

Here a **neigh**, there a **neigh**,

Everywhere a **neigh-neigh**.

Old MacDonald had a farm,
Ee i ee i oh!

Old MacDonald had a farm, **Ee i ee i oh!**
And on his farm he had a dog, **Ee i ee i oh!**
With a **woof-woof** here,
And a **woof-woof** there.

Here a **woof**, there a **woof**,
Everywhere a **woof-woof**.
Old MacDonald had a farm, **Ee i ee i oh!**

Old MacDonald had a farm, **Ee i ee i oh!**
And on his farm he had a frog, **Ee i ee i oh!**
With a **ribbit-ribbit** here,
And a **ribbit-ribbit** there.

Here a **ribbit**, there a **ribbit**,
Everywhere a **ribbit-ribbit**.
Old MacDonald had a farm, **Ee i ee i oh!**

Old MacDonald had a farm, **Ee i ee i oh!**
And on his farm he had a chicken, **Ee i ee i oh!**
With a **cluck-cluck** here,
And a **cluck-cluck** there.

Here a cluck, there a cluck,
Everywhere a cluck-cluck.
Old MacDonald had a farm, Ee i ee i oh!

Old MacDonald had a farm, **Ee i ee i oh!**

And on his farm he had a duck, **Ee i ee i oh!**

With a **quack-quack** here,

And a **quack-quack** there.

Here a **quack**, there a **quack**,
Everywhere a **quack-quack**.
Old MacDonald had a farm, **Ee i ee i oh!**

Old MacDonald had a farm, **Ee i ee i oh!**

And on his farm he had lots of animals, **Ee i ee i oh!**

And they made **noise** here,

And they made **noise** there.

Here a **noise**, there a **noise**,

Everywhere there's **noisy noise**.

Old MacDonald had a farm, and so he formed a **band!**